For my eighth-grade English teacher, Mr. John Weiner,
who has always believed in me and in the power of good books.
—Jane

Copyright © 1999 Children's Television Workshop (CTW). Sesame Street Muppets © 1999
The Jim Henson Company. All rights reserved under International and Pan-American
Copyright Conventions. Published in the United States by Random House, Inc., and
simultaneously in Canada by Random House of Canada Limited, Toronto, in conjunction with
Children's Television Workshop. Sesame Street, the Sesame Street sign, and CTW Books are
trademarks and service marks of Children's Television Workshop.

Library of Congress Cataloging-in-Publication Data:
Vecchio, Jane.   Sesame Street fairy tales / adapted by Jane Vecchio ;
illustrated by Tom Leigh and Joel Schick.   p.   cm.
SUMMARY: A collection of twelve popular fairy tales with a twist, updated and
featuring characters from "Sesame Street."
ISBN 0-679-89411-X (trade) — ISBN 0-679-99411-4 (lib. bdg.)
1. Fairy tales. [1. Fairy tales. 2. Folklore.] I. Leigh, Tom, ill.   II. Schick, Joel, ill.
III. Title. PZ8.V264Se 1999 [398.21]—dc21 [E] 98-45498

www.randomhouse.com/ctwbooks   www.sesamestreet.com

Printed in the United States of America   November 1999   10 9 8 7 6 5 4 3 2 1

RANDOM HOUSE and colophon are registered trademarks of Random House, Inc.

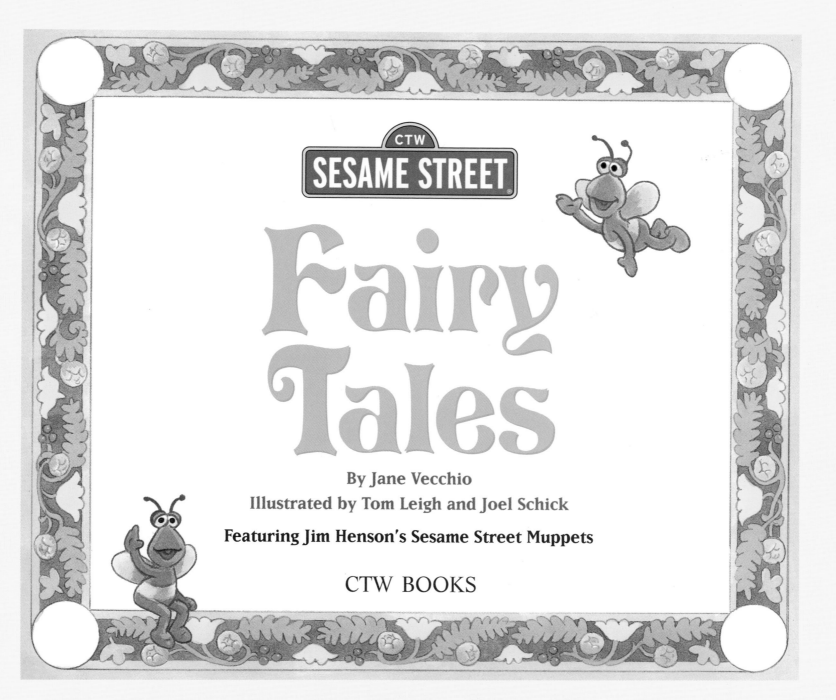

CTW

SESAME STREET®

Fairy Tales

By Jane Vecchio

Illustrated by Tom Leigh and Joel Schick

Featuring Jim Henson's Sesame Street Muppets

CTW BOOKS

Contents

Little Red Riding Hood   8

Tom Thumb   12

The Sword in the Stone   16

Goldilocks and the Three Bears   20

Elmo and the Beanstalk   24

Sleeping Beauty   30

Hansel and Gretel   34

The Princess and the Pea   40

The Twiddlebugs and the Shoemakers   44

Rapunzel   48

Cinderella   52

Pinocchio   58

Little Red Riding Hood

 One day, a little girl was getting ready to go to her grandmother's house. Her name was Rosita, but everyone called her Little Red Riding Hood because she always wore a red cape with a red hood.

Little Red Riding Hood's mother gave her a basket of good things to eat and a get-well card for her grandmother, who had a cold. "Be careful on the way to Abuelita's and give her a big hug from me," said her mother. (Some people call their grandmothers Grandma, others call them Nana, and others have different names altogether. In Little Red Riding Hood's family, Grandmother was called Abuelita.)

Little Red Riding Hood took the big basket and began walking to her grandmother's house, which wasn't too far through the forest. She was happy to be out in the fresh air and sunshine, and she began singing a song as she walked.

Suddenly, a very big wolf with a blue face, a big nose, and big teeth stepped out from behind a tree and startled Little Red Riding Hood. *"Ai ai ai!"* she yelled, and began to run.

"Hold on there!" said the wolf. "No need to run. I am a *friendly* wolf."

"Yeah, sure," said Little Red Riding Hood, but she stopped running when she got far enough away to feel safe. "I am just walking to my grandmother's house and did not expect to be terrified by a big wolf on the way. You may be friendly, but you are scary, too!"

"Accept my apologies," said the wolf, smiling his best wolf smile. "I do not want

to scare you or keep you from going to...where did you say you were going?"

"To my grandmother's," replied Little Red Riding Hood. "She's not feeling well, and I have this basket of good food for her. Her house is across the next stream, and then you take a left at the third oak tree. Well, I must be going now. *¡Adiós!*"

But the wolf was already gone. Little Red Riding Hood went on her way, glad that she had kept far away from that big bad wolf.

Little Red Riding Hood crossed the stream and turned left at the third oak tree and came at last to her grandmother's house. "*Hola*, Abuelita. I have brought you some good things to eat and a get-well card."

"That's nice, dear," said Little Red Riding Hood's grandmother from her bed. Little Red Riding Hood came closer and then stopped.

"Abuelita?" she asked, feeling that something was not quite right. "It is dark here. May I turn on a light?"

"No, no!" said Abuelita. "The light hurts my eyes. Just come closer to me!"

"Hmm," thought Little Red Riding Hood to herself. "This Abuelita does not look like my Abuelita!"

"Abuelita, what big ears you have!" said Little Red Riding Hood.

"All the better to hear you with, my dear," said the wolf, for that is who was really in Abuelita's bed.

"What big eyes you have!" said Little Red Riding Hood.

"All the better to see you with," said the wolf.

"What a big nose you have!" said Little Red Riding Hood.

10

"All the better to smell that basket of food you brought me," said the wolf, drooling a little bit.

"And what big teeth you have!" said Little Red Riding Hood.

"ALL THE BETTER TO EAT YOU WITH!" yelled the wolf, and he jumped out of bed.

But Little Red Riding Hood just stood there. "Forget it, wolf!" she said.

"Oh, gee," said the wolf. "I wanted to be so scary that you'd run out the door." He looked very downhearted.

"And you thought that if I ran out the door, you'd get to eat all these treats I brought in my basket for my Abuelita," said Little Red Riding Hood. She opened the closet, where she found her grandmother hiding from the wolf. "I'll bet you wouldn't even have shared the food with my Abuelita!"

"Um, well, er, no," said the wolf, and he began to cry from shame.

"Listen, wolf," said Little Red Riding Hood. "Being mean and scary is not the way to get what you want. You need to learn to be polite and to ask nicely when you want something, and to share with others. You can share this delicious food with my Abuelita, but only if you show good manners!"

"*Gracias*—I mean, *por favor*—I mean, *sí*—I mean, gee, thanks!" said the wolf. Then he and Abuelita and Little Red Riding Hood had lunch together, eating all the good things in Red Riding Hood's basket.

Tom Thumb

 Once upon a time, there lived a husband and wife who wanted, more than anything, to have a baby. But year after year went by and no baby came.

"Oh, how I want a baby," said the woman. "I'd take any kind of baby at all. I'd take a baby with green bumps all over him. I'd take a baby with ears as big as rowboats. I'd take a baby who was as tiny as my thumb!"

"Yep," said the man, "me, too. I'd love any baby very much!"

Well, one day, the woman did give birth to a baby. He didn't have green bumps all over him. He didn't have ears as big as rowboats. But he *was* as tiny as a thumb! And his parents were as happy as could be. They named him Tom Thumb, and they all became a family.

No matter how many broccoli spears he ate, no matter how many jumping jacks he did, no matter how many chewable vitamins he chewed, Tom Thumb never grew any bigger than a thumb. He was tiny, but he was happy—except for one thing. He wanted to have adventures!

One day, Tom Thumb was helping his father take their horse into the barn for the night. Tom was sitting in the horse's ear, telling it where to go. When he jumped out of the horse's ear onto the ground, two strangers saw him and said, "Hey! Who is this tiny person? He's the strangest thing we've seen! Let's take him with us and we'll put him in our circus."

Tom's father didn't think about it for even a split second. "No!" he said. "My son stays here with his family."

But Tom had a different idea. "Let me go and have adventures. I'll come back soon, I promise." And so Tom's father let him go.

On the way to the circus, Tom rode on the hat of one of the strangers. From his perch, he could look out over the fields, say hello to the field mice, and watch the Twiddlebugs light up the night sky. Then Tom heard one of the strangers say to the other, "Hey! Let's get this little guy to sneak into the rich circus master's tent and steal all his money! No one will see him, and we'll be rich!" And the other stranger laughed a mean laugh.

Tom thought and thought about what he would do. When they all reached the circus, the strangers showed Tom how to slip under the flap of the circus master's tent. Then Tom was supposed to steal the money. Tom did slip under the flap, and he did find the money, but then he did something unexpected. He yelled in the loudest voice he could, "SO, YOU WANT TO STEAL ALL OF THIS MONEY?"

The circus master woke up! The two strangers ran away! The money was saved! And Tom slipped back outside. "Whew," he said. "I'm glad that's over. It's wrong to steal things! That's not my kind of adventure."

Just then, Tom felt something snuffling, sniffling, snarfling on the back of his neck. He turned around and saw a big gray wrinkled trunk. The big gray wrinkled trunk was attached to a big gray wrinkled elephant, who thought Tom was a peanut! "Whoa!" yelled Tom, and he ran as fast as he could through the circus grounds.

Tom ran and ran, but his problems just got worse. He landed in a lion's food dish and almost became the lion's lunch. He nearly got stepped on by 427 people trying to get good seats for the circus. Then someone thought he was a piece of popcorn and tossed him up in the air. He landed in a big orange drink!

"This is really not my kind of adventure," he thought as he ran away from the circus. Now Tom was in a dark field in the middle of nowhere. "How will I get home?" he wondered, and he began to cry.

All at once, a bright light appeared behind him. Then another light appeared. And another. Tom stopped crying and looked up. "Twiddlebugs!" he said. "May I have a ride home?"

"Anytime," said the Twiddlebugs, and Tom jumped onto the back of a Twiddlebutterfly named Timmy. They twiddled up, up, up into the night sky, flying home. Tom loved every minute of it.

"Now, this is my kind of adventure!" he said. "And riding in my horse's ear is an adventure, too. There are plenty of adventures I can have close to home." Tom couldn't wait to hug and kiss his parents again and tell them all about the circus and plan new adventures right in his own backyard. And as soon as he got home, that's exactly what he did.

The Sword in the Stone

 Once upon a time, there was a kingdom that was in big trouble. People were mad and sad all the time, and there wasn't enough to eat. And worst of all, there wasn't a king to take charge!

One snowy day, when the citizens were feeling their maddest and saddest, there suddenly appeared in the middle of town a huge stone with a big, shiny sword stuck in it. On the stone were these words: WHOEVER CAN PULL THE SWORD FROM THIS STONE IS THE RIGHTFUL KING OF THIS LAND.

The people cheered up when they heard this news. A new king at last! They all lined up to try to pull the sword from the stone. All the weightlifters, with their monster muscles, and all the ballplayers who could dunk a basketball without jumping gave it a try. And all those skinny folks who could dance the limbo, all those little ones who could crawl under the smallest tables and chairs, and even those who were shy gave it a try. But nobody could pull the sword from the stone. Day after day passed, and lines of hopeful people tried their best to free it, but still the sword stayed stuck where it was.

Watching all this were a wise old teacher named Merlin and his young student, Arthur. Arthur had learned all sorts of things from Merlin: how to read and write, how to have fun, how to cooperate, and how to plant a garden. Arthur knew a lot, but he didn't know one important thing—how to have faith in himself.

"Gee, Merlin," said Arthur as they watched person after person try and fail to

pull the sword from the stone. "I could never do that!"

"Why not?" asked Merlin. "Go on, give it a try!"

"Nah, I don't want to," Arthur replied. "I'm afraid people will laugh at me. I might make a funny grunting noise! I might pull too hard and fall in the snow!"

"It's scary to take a chance, isn't it?" Merlin said. "I promise that I won't laugh at you. And anyway, how do you know what you can do until you try?"

Arthur sighed. He knew that he had learned a lot from Merlin, but was it enough to give him courage? Arthur closed his eyes for a moment and squeezed Merlin's hand. Then he joined the line of people waiting their turn at the stone.

When Arthur's turn came, he was nervous. Some people did laugh at him. "Hey, look at that big bird! What is he going to do, use his yellow feathers to pull out that big sword? Ha ha ha!"

Arthur pretended not to hear. He looked at Merlin. Merlin nodded at him and said again, "How do you know what you can do until you try?"

Arthur walked up to the big sword. He took hold of its shiny handle. He braced his foot on the stone. He took a deep breath, and he pulled.

Arthur pulled the sword right out of that stone! The sword came out so fast that Arthur fell backward in the snow! But no one laughed. No one said a word. Everyone stood there with their mouths wide open, except Merlin, who just smiled. Then all the people started to yell and cheer and jump for joy. "Our new king is here! Long live our king!"

At first Arthur could not believe it himself. And then he felt happy and proud. "I'll be a good king," he promised. "I'll teach you what Merlin has taught me. We can all learn in school, and have fun, and cooperate with each other instead of getting mad. And we'll grow a big garden in town so no one will be hungry again!"

"Yay! Yay!" cried the people. And Merlin just kept smiling.

Goldilocks and the Three Bears

 Once, in a bear forest, in a bear house, at a bear table, sat three bears on bear chairs. There was a big Papa Bear with a big green tie, a medium-size Mama Bear with a medium-size hat, and a little Baby Bear with a little baseball cap. The bears were just about to eat the porridge Papa Bear had made.

Baby Bear sprinkled some cinnamon on his porridge, grabbed his spoon, and put a big spoonful in his mouth. *"Ouch! Ouch!"*

The porridge was way too hot! Baby Bear had burned his little tongue. The three bears decided to take a walk outside while their porridge cooled off.

While the bears were gone, a little girl named Goldilocks happened by the bear house. She had been out walking, and walking always made her hungry. From the bear house, she smelled a most delicious smell. Her stomach growled and growled! The door of the house was open, so she went right in.

"Yoo-hoo!" cried Goldilocks, but nobody answered.

The first thing Goldilocks did was head straight for that yummy-smelling porridge. She tried the big bowl, but the porridge was way too hot. Then she tried the medium-size bowl, and that porridge was sort of too hot. Then she tried the little bowl, and the porridge was just right, so she ate it all up.

Now that her stomach had stopped growling, Goldilocks looked around the house. "Cool," she said. "I'm going to explore!"

Goldilocks watched some television. She tried on some skates. She found a rubber ducky and gave it a swim in the bathroom sink. Then she saw three chairs.

She tried to sit on the big chair, but it was way too big. She tried the medium-size chair, but it was sort of too big. Then she tried the little chair, and it seemed just right. But suddenly, Goldilocks crashed to the floor. She had broken the chair!

"Oops! Oh, well, I'm sleepy anyway," she said, and went off to find the bedroom. The first bed she tried was way too big. The medium-size bed was sort of too big. But the little bed was just right, and Goldilocks tucked herself in for a nap and fell sound asleep.

When the three bears came home, things seemed not quite right. Mama Bear said, "Hmm. We'll get to the bottom of this!"

Papa Bear walked over to his porridge bowl. "Someone's been tasting my porridge!" he said in his big voice.

"Someone's been tasting *my* porridge," said Mama Bear in her medium-size voice.

"Someone's been tasting *my* porridge—and it's all gone!" cried Baby Bear in his little voice.

The bears noticed that the television was on. They saw their skates on the floor. They found the rubber ducky in the sink. "Hmm," said Mama Bear. "I am not amused by this. It looks as if a bunch of messy monsters have been in here!" Then the bears saw their chairs.

"Someone's been sitting in my chair!" said Papa in his big voice.

"Someone's been sitting in *my* chair," said Mama Bear in her medium-size voice.

"And someone's been sitting in *my* chair, and it's all smashed!" cried Baby Bear in his little voice.

Finally, the bears went to the bedroom to look for that bunch of messy monsters.

"Someone's been sleeping in my bed!" said Papa in his big voice.

"Someone's been sleeping in *my* bed," said Mama Bear in her medium-size voice.

"And someone's been sleeping in *my* bed, and there she is!" cried Baby Bear in his little voice, and he yanked the blanket right off Goldilocks.

"*Eeeeeeeeeeeeek!*" screamed Goldilocks, who had never seen a real live bear before, and she jumped out of bed and ran out of the house.

So the bears had to clean up after Goldilocks, who was really just as messy as a bunch of messy monsters. And while they were cleaning, their porridge got ice-cold. Papa made another batch of porridge, and the bears sat down to eat.

Baby Bear sprinkled some cinnamon on his porridge, grabbed his spoon, and put a big spoonful in his mouth. *"Ouch! Ouch!"*

And what do you think happened next?

Elmo and the Beanstalk

 A long, long time ago, in a tiny little house with hardly any furniture, hardly any clothes, and hardly any food, a little monster named Elmo lived with his mother. One day, Elmo's mother said sadly, "We must sell our cow to get some money so we can eat. Please take her to town and get the best price you can!"

So Elmo and the cow went to town. When they got there, Elmo saw a store with a big sign that said COWS R US! As he was going into the store, a man said, "If you sell me your cow, I'll give you these," and he held out a handful of beans.

Now, these weren't the ordinary kind of baked brown beans you eat with hot dogs, and they weren't the kind of green beans you eat because your parents make you eat them. These beans were beautiful, shiny, and all the colors of the rainbow.

"Elmo loves these beans!" giggled Elmo, and he gave the man the cow for the beautiful, shiny, rainbow-colored beans.

When Elmo's mother heard about COWS R US! and saw the little pile of beans, she was not happy. She threw the beans out the window and said, "How can we buy food with these silly little beans?!" Then she sent Elmo to his room.

"Elmo's sorry," he said, and cried himself to sleep.

But that night, something amazing happened. The beautiful, shiny, rainbow-colored beans grew roots in the ground outside the window. A beanstalk started growing out of the ground, up to the sky. It kept growing and growing until it was as

strong as the strongest ladder and as thick as a tree trunk.

The next morning, Elmo woke up and saw the amazing beanstalk.

"Elmo's going to climb this thing," he said, and he began climbing, giggling all the way because the leaves tickled his tummy.

When he got to the top, way up in the clouds, Elmo saw a huge castle. Elmo crept into the castle and found himself in a huge kitchen. He looked around in amazement. Everything was so much bigger than his things at home! The table was as tall as a truck. The sink was as deep as a swimming pool. Someone had dropped a spoon on the floor, and the scoop of the spoon was as big as a bathtub.

As Elmo climbed over the spoon, he heard a pounding *thump thump* noise. He looked up. There at the huge table, making a huge pie with apples as big as beach balls, was the biggest woman Elmo had ever seen. She had bright orange bushy hair as wild as a bunch of orange jump ropes, and hands as big as kites.

Then Elmo heard a whooshing *zroom zroom* noise. He looked across the room. There in a huge chair, taking a huge nap, was the hugest man Elmo had ever seen. He had bushy eyebrows the size of furry dogs, and feet as long as rowboats. And under this huge man's feet was a bag of golden eggs. He was a giant! Elmo was in a giant's castle! And Elmo was beginning to be a little bit scared.

The giant's wife bent down to pick up the spoon from the floor, and she saw Elmo. She jumped and yelped in surprise!

"Don't be scared," said Elmo. "Elmo is just a poor little monster who has no money to buy something to eat."

"Oh, you poor little furry monster," said the giant's wife. "You can have some of our golden eggs. We have more than we need!" But just then, the giant began to wake up.

"*Snort, snuff, snootch,*" said the giant, stretching and yawning. And then he woke all the way up.

"Fee, fi, fo, fum, I smell the feet of a furry one! When I catch him in my place, I will shake his furry face!" he roared, and began looking all over the kitchen for Elmo. But the giant's wife hid Elmo in the pie she was making. When the giant went into another room to look for Elmo, the giant's wife gave the bag of golden eggs to Elmo and helped him out of the pie. Elmo ran all the way to the beanstalk and slid down to his house, giggling all the way as the leaves tickled his tummy.

Elmo and his mother lived for a long time on the money they got from selling the golden eggs. But when the golden eggs were all gone, Elmo knew just what to do. He climbed back up the beanstalk, giggling all the way because the leaves tickled his tummy.

Once again, Elmo found himself in the giant's kitchen. And once again, the giant was taking a huge nap, with his huge feet on a bag of golden eggs that was twice as big as the other one had been. But this time, near the bag was a goose, who was laying even more golden eggs.

Elmo crept over to the goose and began petting her. Just then, the giant began to wake up.

"Snort, snuff, snootch," said the giant, stretching and yawning. And then he woke all the way up. "Fee, fi, fo, fum, I smell the feet of a furry one!" he roared. "When I catch him in my place, I will shake his furry face!" Elmo grabbed the goose and began to run, and the giant ran after him!

Elmo ran and ran as fast as he could, holding the goose tightly. Behind him, he could hear the *BOOM! BOOM! BOOM!* of the giant's footsteps. Elmo reached the beanstalk and slid down it as fast as he could. He slid so fast he didn't have time to giggle.

When he got to the bottom, Elmo began to chop down the beanstalk with an ax. Way, way up above, he could hear the giant at the top of the beanstalk. "Fee, fi, fo, fum, I smell the feet of a furry one! When I catch him in my place, I will shake his furry face!" Just as the giant put out his huge foot to climb down, Elmo chopped the beanstalk all the way through, and it fell out of the clouds onto the ground. Way, way up above, he heard the giant yelling. But this time, he was yelling, "Oh, rats!"

Elmo and his mother lived happily ever after because they knew that they would always have enough furniture, clothes, and food, thanks to the goose who laid golden eggs. And the goose was happy to live in a house where people weren't yelling all the time.

Sleeping Beauty

 Once upon a time, in a faraway kingdom, a king and queen had a baby daughter. They were so happy with baby Zoe that they decided to celebrate with a big party.

The king sent special invitations to the most special monsters of the land. But the king and queen had only twelve special golden plates for the table, and there were thirteen special monsters. So one of the monsters was not invited.

When the day of the party came, the guests had fun eating a cake that had ZOE written on it in pink icing. They drank special orange Zoe punch. They sang, "Zoe, Zoe, whoop-de-doo!" for hours and hours.

The twelve monsters at the party made wonderful wishes for baby Zoe. One monster wished Zoe a lifetime of happiness. Another monster wished she would be good in math at school. Another wished her lots and lots of cookies! (You probably know which monster that was.) Baby Zoe was getting the best wishes ever!

Then, all of a sudden, the palace door crashed open, and someone charged in. It was the monster who had not been invited! It was a grouch!

"Party, shmarty," said the grouch. "This place stinks. Who wants all this crummy cake and icky punch, anyway? Not me. That song you're singing is dumb, too. Oh, and by the way, that baby Zoe has the face of a toad!"

The crowd gasped. This monster was a major grouch! "I'm not going to make a nice wish because I'm a grouch," he said. "So here's a grouchy wish instead." The

crowd gasped again as the grouch continued. "One day, this toad-faced baby will cut her finger on a pair of scissors, and then she'll sleep for a hundred years! And you will all fall asleep, too!"

And with that, the grouch crashed back out the door of the palace.

Now, the king and queen were pretty worried about this, so they put up a big sign in the kingdom that said NO SCISSORS ALLOWED. Because of this, everyone in the kingdom had to use knives or their teeth to cut things. After a few years, they forgot about the grouch and his grouchy wish, but they remembered not to use scissors.

One day, Zoe (who was not a baby anymore) was playing in the castle when she found a dusty old door. She opened it and stepped inside. There she saw something she had never seen before. She saw a furry monster cutting paper with a strange thing that looked like two little knives with round handles joined together.

"May I try that?" she asked. "It looks like fun."

The monster (who was really the grouch) handed her the scissors. As Zoe tried to put her fingers in the handles, she cut her furry finger a tiny bit. "Ooh," she said. She got very sleepy and went to lie down on her bed.

Zoe fell asleep. The king and queen fell asleep, too. In fact, everyone in the kingdom fell asleep. All the Twiddlebugs, all the people, all the monsters, all the dogs and cats and worms, and even the trees and flowers fell asleep.

Near and far, the story of sleeping Zoe was told. Only now she was called

Sleeping Beauty. People were scared of the kingdom where everyone was fast asleep. Everyone was scared—except for Prince Elmo.

Prince Elmo decided to go to the sleeping kingdom to see if he could wake up Sleeping Beauty. "Elmo's not afraid," he said, and off he went. When he got to the palace, he went up to Sleeping Beauty's room and tried to figure out how to wake her. He tried calling her name. He tried poking her nose. He even tried jumping up and down on the mattress twenty-three times. But still Sleeping Beauty slept.

Then Elmo had an idea.

He tickled her!

"Hee hee hee!" said Sleeping Beauty. She woke up at last. At the same time, everyone in the kingdom woke up. The king and queen, the Twiddlebugs, all the people, all the monsters, all the dogs and cats and worms, and even the trees and flowers woke up. The grouch woke up, too, and came to the castle to see Sleeping Beauty (who was now just Zoe again).

"Sometimes even a grouch has to say he's sorry," said the grouch. "I was just grouchy because I didn't get invited to your dumb party."

So the king and queen decided to celebrate with another big party. Only this time, they bought enough special golden party plates for all the monsters in the land.

Hansel and Gretel

Once upon a time, a brother and sister named Hansel and Gretel got into trouble for being naughty. Their parents sent them to their room *without dessert.* (They must have done something pretty bad.)

So Hansel and Gretel decided to run away from home. They planned to go into the deep, dark woods nearby. But Gretel was a little bit worried.

"Gee, we don't really want to run away from home forever," she said. "I know! Let's fill our pockets with shiny little white stones and drop them as we walk. Then we can find our way home again!" Hansel agreed that this was a good plan.

The next day, Hansel and Gretel ran away from home, into the deep, dark woods. They walked and walked. They walked some more. All that walking made them tired and hungry, and they began to feel bad about being naughty in the first place and about worrying their parents. So they decided to go back home. They followed the trail of shiny little white stones they had dropped along the way, and they were home before dark—before their parents even knew they had been gone.

Well, Hansel and Gretel were always getting into one kind of mischief or another, and it seemed that they got sent to their room every single day. So one day, they decided to run away from home again. But they had used all the shiny little white stones, so Hansel stuffed bread crumbs in his pocket instead.

Hansel and Gretel went into the deep, dark woods. They walked and walked. They walked some more. All that walking made them tired and hungry, and they began

to feel bad about getting into more trouble and about worrying their parents. So they decided to go home again.

"Let's follow the trail of bread crumbs," said Gretel, and they turned around.

But there *were* no bread crumbs! There wasn't a single bread crumb in sight. Instead, they saw some very happy birds licking their beaks. The birds had eaten the bread crumb trail!

"Oh, nooo!" said Hansel and Gretel, and they began to cry.

The only thing to do was keep walking, and so they did. They walked and walked and walked some more into the deep, dark woods. By now, they were very tired and very hungry.

Suddenly, they came to a clearing and saw the most amazing sight. It was a pretty little house made of delightful things to eat! The walls were made of gingerbread, and the roof was made of cookies. Candy canes framed the door, and jellybeans were stuck all over the yummy-looking house.

"Oh, boy, oh, boy!" said Hansel and Gretel, and they ran over to the house and began to eat it. Hansel started to chew on a piece of a gingerbread wall, and Gretel licked a lollipop flower. The house was not only pretty, it was *delicious!*

All at once, from inside the house, they heard a loud voice. "Me hear someone eating gingerbread house! Who there?"

Oops! Hansel and Gretel had to think fast. "It's just the wind blowing," called Gretel.

"Oh, okay," said the loud voice from inside the house. "As long as nobody eating gingerbread house." So Hansel and Gretel kept munching on the house.

They must have been munching and crunching pretty loudly. "Me not like this!" said the voice from inside the house, and then the candy door banged open. Standing there was a big blue furry monster!

"Cowabunga! Not nice to eat monster's delicious house!" the monster said.

Hansel and Gretel said they were sorry about eating the monster's house. They explained that they were lost and very, very hungry.

"Oh! Why you not say so in first place?" said the monster. Then he brought Hansel and Gretel a pitcher of nice lemonade and a plate of cookies. But soon the lemonade and cookies were all gone.

"Me still hungry!" the monster said. Hansel and Gretel were still hungry, too. They waited to see what the monster would do. He looked up and down. He looked left and right. He looked at his gingerbread and candy house. Then he started to shake and quake and jump up and down. "COWABUNGA! WE EAT HOUSE!"

He tore a candy-cane picture frame off the wall and chomped it up!

Hansel and Gretel joined right in. First, they ate all the furniture inside the gingerbread house. Into their mouths went the licorice chairs and the peppermint-stick tables. "Mmmm!" said Hansel and Gretel and the monster, wiping their faces.

Then, without even pausing for a minute, they ate all the cookie tiles off the roof and the icing trim, too. "COOKIE! COOKIE!" yelled the monster as the crumbs flew all over the place. Hansel and Gretel had never had such delicious food, and they stuffed everything into their mouths as fast as they could. They even yelled, "COOKIE!" a few times, just like the monster!

Were Hansel and Gretel and the monster full then? Oh, no! They began to eat the windows, and the walls, and the doors, too. Hansel and Gretel and the monster ate all of it…

And then they ate up the cotton-candy carpets and the peanut-brittle floors, too!

Finally, they stopped eating and looked around. Where the gingerbread house had been was now a bare spot. The chimney was gone. The roof and the walls were gone. Every single piece of furniture was gone. Even the gumdrop flowers and bushes from around the house were gone. They had eaten everything.

Hansel and Gretel looked at each other and then at the monster. They were worried that he might be mad that his gingerbread house was all gone. The monster *did* have a funny look on his face, kind of a scrunched-up, puckered-up look. Hansel and Gretel were very worried now. Then the monster scrunched up his face even more and said, *"BUUUURRRRPPPP!!!* That house good!"

Well, Hansel and Gretel and the monster laughed so hard that they *all* began burping. *"Burp! Burp! BURP!"* They agreed that the gingerbread house was the best-tasting house in the whole wide world, and that Hansel and Gretel could come back any time they wanted to visit the monster in his next house (*if* they had their parents' permission, of course).

And with that, the monster pointed Hansel and Gretel on the path to their house, and they went on their way home, waving good-bye to their furry and full friend.

Soon they were safely home.

"Let's be good from now on so that we never get sent to our room without dessert," Hansel said to Gretel.

"Good idea," answered Gretel.

And they never ran away from home again.

The Princess and the Pea

 Once upon a time, there was a picky prince named Ernie who wanted to marry a real, live, genuine princess. No pretend princess would do! So he traveled all over his kingdom looking for a bride.

On his travels, Prince Ernie found many pretty girls, many smart girls, many talented girls, many nice girls, and many girls who were pretty, smart, talented, *and* nice all at the same time. But he wasn't satisfied. He found something wrong with every single girl.

"This girl has a rubber ducky that isn't yellow," he said. "That one over there knows more funny jokes than I do. The girl I met yesterday doesn't like pepperoni on her pizza. And besides, not one of them is a real, live, genuine princess." Boy, was this prince ever picky! So he went home, very discouraged because he couldn't find anyone to marry.

One stormy night, when the rain pounded on the windows and the wind rattled the roof, Prince Ernie and his family heard a *Bang! Bang! Bang!* on the door of the castle. When they opened the door, they found a cold, tired, and very wet girl standing outside.

"I am Princess Prairie Dawn, and I would be very grateful if you would let me sleep here tonight," she said.

"Oh, sure," thought Prince Ernie. "A real, live, genuine princess at our door?"

His mother the queen and his father the king also wondered if the girl was telling

the truth. They invited her to spend the night in their guest bedroom, but they decided to give her a test.

"We'll put something under her mattress," said the queen. "If she's a true princess, her skin will be so delicate that she will feel it and won't be able to sleep a wink."

"But what should we put under the mattress?" asked the king. He turned to his trusted adviser, who was standing nearby.

"COOKIE!" yelled the adviser, Sir Cookie Monster.

"I don't think so. Not practical at all. Too many crumbs," answered the king.

"COOKIE! COOKIE! COOKIE!" yelled Sir Cookie Monster. "Me want cookie!"

"Oh, go into the kitchen and find us something more practical, please," said the queen. Sir Cookie Monster went to the kitchen, ate 312 cookies, and then came back with a bowl of raw peas in his paw.

"Perfect!" Prince Ernie said. "Let's make this test super-hard. Let's put twenty mattresses on top of a single little pea. Then this so-called princess will sleep on top of them all. Hee hee hee!"

So the queen and Sir Cookie Monster put one little pea on the bed. On top of the pea they placed twenty mattresses. On top of the mattresses they placed a big, soft comforter, sheets, and a blanket. They went to get the girl, who had dried off and put on some royal pajamas, and they tucked her in for the night.

All night, Prince Ernie laughed to himself. "Hee hee

hee! This girl will turn out to be false like all the others. Only a real, live, genuine princess has skin delicate enough to feel a pea under all those mattresses."

The next morning, the queen, the king, and Prince Ernie waited for Prairie Dawn. When she came down for breakfast, they asked, "How did you sleep last night?"

"I had a terrible night! I tossed and turned and didn't sleep a wink. There was something so hard in my bed that I am black-and-blue all over this morning."

"You are a real, live, genuine princess!" gasped Prince Ernie. "The test worked."

"I told you I was a princess. And hey, what test are you talking about, anyway?" replied Princess Prairie Dawn.

So Prince Ernie, the queen, and the king confessed what they had done. The princess was not too happy at first. She didn't like being tested. And she didn't like the prince's pickiness. But she really loved Prince Ernie anyway, and so she decided to marry him after all.

And amazingly enough, the prince loved her, too—even though her rubber ducky wasn't yellow, she knew more funny jokes than he did, and she really, really didn't like pepperoni on her pizza.

The Twiddlebugs
and the Shoemakers

 "OUCH!" "Look out!" *CRASH!* "Oh, no!"

Those were the sounds coming out of Ernie and Bert's Shoe Shop every day and every night. You see, the two shoemakers wanted to make nice shoes, but they didn't really know how. They dropped tools on each other's feet. They put shoelaces on the bottoms of sneakers. They sewed two shoes together by mistake. Ernie and Bert tried hard, but nobody wanted to buy their shoes. They were very discouraged.

One night, the shoemakers looked around their shop. Cobwebs were all over the empty shelves. All of their weird shoes were gathering dust in the corners.

"I have an idea," said Ernie. "Let's try making shoes for fish so the sand on the bottom of the ocean won't hurt their feet!"

"Oh, Ernie, fish don't wear shoes," said Bert. "Be serious."

"Okay, Bert. How about this? We can make pretend Swiss cheese by cutting little holes in leather, and then we can make pretend sandwiches for people to buy."

"Argh!" said Bert. "I am too worried to joke around. I'm going to sleep!" So Bert and Ernie slept a worried sleep.

The next morning, the shoemakers went into their workroom, expecting to see cobwebs and empty shelves. But they saw something else entirely. They saw rows and

rows of nice new beautiful shoes! For a long time, they stood there with their mouths wide open. How had these shoes appeared?

Ernie and Bert didn't have long to think about this mystery. They were too busy all day selling the nice new beautiful shoes to very happy customers.

The next day, more new shoes appeared. And the next day, it happened again.

That night, Ernie said, "Say, Bert, I have an idea."

"What now, Ernie?" Bert asked.

"Let's hide tonight and see who is leaving these amazing shoes," Ernie suggested.

Bert had to agree that this was a good plan. So late that night, he and Ernie hid behind the big table in the workroom and waited.

They waited until eight. They waited until nine. They waited until ten. They waited until eleven. Nothing happened. Then, when it was midnight and Bert and Ernie were feeling very sleepy, a strange bright light appeared in the windows. Then the strange bright light appeared in the doorway. The light was made by...eighty-four Twiddlebugs!

Ernie and Bert watched as the Twiddlebugs cut beautiful shoe shapes out of leather. They watched as the Twiddlebugs sewed the leather pieces together very, very carefully. They watched as the Twiddlebugs added shoelaces in the right places and put bows on the fancy party shoes and thick soles on the outdoor shoes. As they watched the Twiddlebugs, Ernie and Bert learned how to make nice new beautiful shoes.

"Yippee!" yelled Ernie.

"Yay!" said Bert. They leaped out from behind the table and jumped up and down for joy. But when they yelled and jumped—*WHOOSH!*—all eighty-four Twiddlebugs flew away at once.

"Gee, I think we scared our little friends," said Ernie.

He and Bert began calling to the Twiddlebugs: "Come out! Let us thank you all!" And one by one, the Twiddlebugs came out of hiding.

"You little friends showed us how to make nice new beautiful shoes," said Ernie. "Bert and I never knew how before. Now we can practice and practice and make them ourselves. You have saved Ernie and Bert's Shoe Shop!"

"How can we thank you?" asked Bert.

"You can start practicing right now by making us eighty-four tiny pairs of purple Twiddlebug shoes," said the head Twiddlebug.

And that's exactly what Ernie and Bert did!

Rapunzel

 Once upon a time in a distant land, a woman saw some special golden lettuce that grew in a garden nearby. All day and all night, she looked out her window at this lettuce, and her stomach growled and growled. She couldn't ask for the lettuce because it grew in a garden owned by her neighbor—and that neighbor was a grouch!

The woman's husband was worried. "You are going to have a baby soon, Dear," he said. "You need to eat!"

"The only thing I want to eat is some of that grouch's golden lettuce," she replied. "Nothing else will do. Will you go out tonight and pick some for me?"

Well, the man knew that it was wrong, but he was so worried about his wife that he agreed. That night, he sneaked into the grouch's garden and pulled up some golden lettuce. He took it home, and his wife ate it all up.

"More!" she cried, and so the man went into the grouch's garden the next night.

Just as he was pulling up a big bunch of golden lettuce, he felt a *tap, tap, tap* on his shoulder. He turned around and saw the grouch!

"Listen, buddy, take your stinky hands off my lettuce!" snarled the grouch. "And get your crummy shoes off my carrots, too!"

The man explained that his wife was having a baby and was hungry for the grouch's golden lettuce.

"Hmm," said the grouch. "It might be fun to have a little kid around the place. I

could teach the kid to be a super grouch. I'll let you have all the lettuce you want, but you have to promise me that you'll let me raise the baby to be a grouch."

The man needed the lettuce so badly that he agreed!

When the baby girl was born, she went to live with the grouch. He named her Rapunzel, which was the name of the special golden lettuce in his garden. As Rapunzel grew up, the grouch taught her all kinds of grouchy things. He taught her how to complain and whine and how to make messes and never clean up. He also taught her not to take baths and never to cut her hair. Her hair grew and grew until it was as long as the longest ladder.

Rapunzel stayed in a big, tall tower, filled with grouch trash treasure. When the grouch wanted to visit her, he called up to the high window, "Rapunzel, Rapunzel! Let down your hair!" And then he climbed up her hair to the window of the tower, and he and Rapunzel played with his trash collection.

Rapunzel didn't like living like a grouch. She wanted to sing happy songs. She wanted to take a bath once in a while. And she really, really wanted to cut her hair.

One day, a handsome prince passed the tower and heard the grouch call Rapunzel and climb up her hair. He also saw Rapunzel! This made him curious, so the next day, the prince called up to the tower in a grouchy voice, "Rapunzel, Rapunzel! Let down your hair!" And she did.

When Rapunzel saw the prince instead of the grouch, she was surprised!

The prince was smitten. "Run away with me!" he said. "I will make you happy. I will take care of you, and you won't have to worry about anything."

But Rapunzel had a different idea. "I've spent my whole life up here in this trash tower being told what to do by a grouch," she said. "I'm not going to spend the rest of my life in a castle being told what to do by a prince. I will make my own decisions, thank you!"

When the prince heard this, he fell even more in love with her, and she fell in love with him.

So the prince helped give Rapunzel her very first haircut, and they made a ladder out of her hair. Then they climbed down the ladder and ran away to live happily ever after.

Cinderella

 "Make me some chocolate milk!"

"Give my rubber ducky a bath!"

This is what poor Cinderella heard all day long. She was the littlest of three girls who all lived in the same house. Her two older stepsisters loved to boss her around. Cinderella wanted them to like her and let her play with them, so she did what they said.

If Bertina wanted someone to make her bed, she called for Cinderella because she was too lazy to do it herself.

"Do a good job and maybe we'll play with you later," she sneered at Cinderella. "But remember, I like my top sheet tucked in tight at the bottom, put my teddy monster on my pillow, and I need my favorite blanket or I can't sleep. Is that clear?"

Or if Ernestina had made a big mess with one of her famous experiments, she expected Cinderella to clean it all up. If Cinderella didn't do it, Ernestina would tell their mother that Cinderella had made the mess. So Cinderella would clean up the mud, sand, paint, clay, and pipe cleaners that Ernestina had left all over the bedroom rug. She hoped that Ernestina would play with her later and that they could do experiments together.

The really rotten thing was that even though Cinderella tried so hard to please them, Bertina and Ernestina never, ever played with her. "You don't have time to play,"

they said. "You have too much work to do! And besides, you're too little!" This wasn't fair at all. Cinderella did all the work, got blamed for all the messes, and never got to have any fun.

One day, a big, square envelope arrived in the mail. It was bright yellow and had gold-glitter stars all around the edges. Cinderella read what was written on the front of the envelope: TO ALL THE GIRLS OF THE HOUSE.

Bertina grabbed the yellow envelope away from Cinderella. "Here, let ME read this," she said, and ripped it open. Ernestina and Cinderella leaned over to read what was inside. It was an invitation that said:

> *It is Grover's birthday ball,*
> *So come and party, one and all!*
> *There'll be lots of cake and punch*
> *And also monster-pies to munch.*
> *When the moon is high and bright,*
> *We will dance and play all night!*
> *P.S.—You never know whom you might meet,*
> *So come dressed up from head to feet!*

"Yippee!" said Cinderella.

Bertina and Ernestina laughed at Cinderella. "No way are *you* going to this party, puny. This party is for all the *big* girls of the house only. They just forgot to say that on the invitation. Besides, you have three beds to make and three closets to clean out and three toy chests to organize by color and shape before we get back. Oh, and you don't mind if we wear your new hair bows, do you? Bye!" And they went to get dressed for the party.

Cinderella went into her room, threw herself on her bed, and began to cry. "It's not fair!" she sobbed. Suddenly, a bright light appeared in Cinderella's room, and *poof!* a beautiful little bluish-greenish person with a shining wand and a big smile jumped on Cinderella's bed.

"*¡Hola!* I am your fairy godmother! I am here to help you, because I know that you are sad."

Cinderella was amazed. "How can you help me?" she said. "I am too little to get my own way, and I want to go to the party. I can't even wear my own hair bows!"

"Well, I am here to tell you that being small can be hard, but that doesn't mean you can't have fun. Look at me—I'm small, too! Let's see what we can do about this!"

And the fairy godmother got to work. First, she helped Cinderella clean her own room, but they left Bertina's and Ernestina's rooms all messy. Then the fairy godmother waved her magic wand, and *poof!* Cinderella was wearing the dress of her dreams and a golden crown that was even better than hair bows. The dress had silky white ribbons and layers of shiny pink satin over fluffy petticoats. It was the most wonderful dress Cinderella had ever seen. The golden crown sparkled and shimmered in the light. Then the fairy godmother pointed her magic wand again, and *poof!* Cinderella had a pair of shoes that were so delicate and pretty they looked like glass. Now she was all dressed up and ready to go to the ball.

"But remember," said the fairy godmother, "you must be home from the party before the clock strikes midnight. If you're not back by then, your crown will turn into a pumpkin leaf, your dress will turn into a brown paper bag, and your shoes will turn into mice. *¡Bueno!* Have a wonderful time!"

Cinderella could not believe her eyes when she arrived at the ball. Everywhere she looked, there were people and monsters having fun!

Well, Cinderella jumped right in and had the time of her life. She drank some blue punch that tasted just like ripe blueberries. She had a big piece of pink birthday cake and ate four monster-pies.

Cinderella also met many new friends at the party, and saw some she already knew. She and Prairie Dawn played stick-the-frown-on-the-paper-grouch, and everyone laughed when Prairie Dawn almost stuck the real Oscar by mistake.

Cinderella and Big Bird danced the Funky Chicken. They flapped their arms and stamped their feet. After the dance was over, Grover gave Big Bird and Cinderella the Best Dancers prize. (Oh, boy, were Bertina and Ernestina jealous!)

All night, people stopped Cinderella and said, "Your dress and crown and shoes are so beautiful!" She felt very pretty and very grown-up. It was the best party ever, and the very best part was that Cinderella wasn't too little for it at all!

Cinderella was having so much fun that she lost track of time. Suddenly, she heard a clock begin to strike the hour. One...two...three, it chimed. Oh, no! It was midnight!

"Okay, you got it, buddy," the cricket said. "With my cricket magic, I'll make you a real boy. Here's the catch, though. You can't ever, ever tell a lie." Then the cricket hopped away before Pinocchio could ask him any questions.

The next morning, Geppetto was feeling sad. He was still lonely. He picked Pinocchio up off the shelf and said, "I guess you're really just a block of wood."

"I am not a blockhead!" said Pinocchio.

"*Aaack!*" yelped Geppetto, and he dropped Pinocchio on the floor. Geppetto watched in amazement as Pinocchio stood up, brushed off his pants, and said, "I am a boy! I want to go to school and learn to ride a bike and eat spaghetti with tomato sauce. But most of all, I want to be with you so you will never be lonely again."

Geppetto was very surprised, but then he was very happy, too. He and Pinocchio talked and had fun and went places together. Neither one was lonely anymore.

Everything was fine until one day when Geppetto came home to find all his woodcarving tools on the floor. "Were you playing with my tools, Pinocchio?" he asked.

"Nope, no way, not a chance," said Pinocchio. Then a strange thing happened. Pinocchio's round, red nose turned bright yellow and began to grow. It grew and grew until it looked like a big banana on his face! When Pinocchio told a lie, his nose told the truth by growing.

Pinocchio was ashamed of himself. "I'm sorry, Geppetto," he said. Then he cleaned up the tools.

One day a few months later, Geppetto's neighbor came to see him. In the neighbor's hand was a baseball. "Someone hit this ball through my window and broke the glass," he said.

"Was it you, Pinocchio?" asked Geppetto.

"Nope, no way, not a chance," said Pinocchio. But his nose grew like a banana before the words were even out of his mouth!

So Pinocchio helped the neighbor clean up the broken glass, and he paid for a new window out of his allowance.

A few months after that, Pinocchio watched television one night and forgot to do his homework. The next day, his teacher asked, "Did you forget to do your homework?"

Pinocchio looked at the teacher and said, "Nope, no way, not a chance!" As you can imagine, his nose turned into the biggest, yellowest banana. All the other kids laughed and laughed! Pinocchio covered his banana nose and ran all the way home, crying. He found Geppetto and told him the whole story.

Geppetto hugged Pinocchio, and then he asked him, "Have you learned your lesson?"

Pinocchio sniffled and said, "Yes, I have. I'm sorry, and I won't ever tell a lie again. I love you, Geppetto!" And Pinocchio's nose became round and red the way Geppetto had made it, and never grew into a banana again.